Tommy & T̶ Go to the Zoo

Biblical Lessons for the Tiny Theologian

Written by Leticia Soto

Illustrated by Jason Velázquez

Xulon Press
2301 Lucien Way #415
Maitland, FL 32751
407.339.4217
www.xulonpress.com

Unless otherwise indicated, Scripture quotations taken from the International Children's Bible (ICB) The Holy Bible, International Children's Bible® Copyright© 1986, 1988, 1999, 2015 by Tommy Nelson™, a division of Thomas Nelson. Used by permission

Printed in the United States of America.

ISBN-13: 978-1-54566-195-6

This book is dedicated to:

Stephanie, Joel, Luis, Israel, Gideon, Lucia, Thomas, Rebekah and Samuel who are the babies that have inspired my life for close to 30 years. Thank you for all the joys, laughter, and moments you all have invested in my life. I am so happy that I have been able to be a witness as you have grown or are growing.

Hi, my name is Tommy and I am five years old. On some weekends I go to my Titi's house for a sleep-over.

Titi is my aunt. I love her a lot! After I brush my teeth and put on my PJ's, we imagine stuff before I go to bed. Then we say a prayer.

"Titi, where is our imagination taking us today?"
"I think we should go to a zoo adventure."
"Yay! I love animals!"

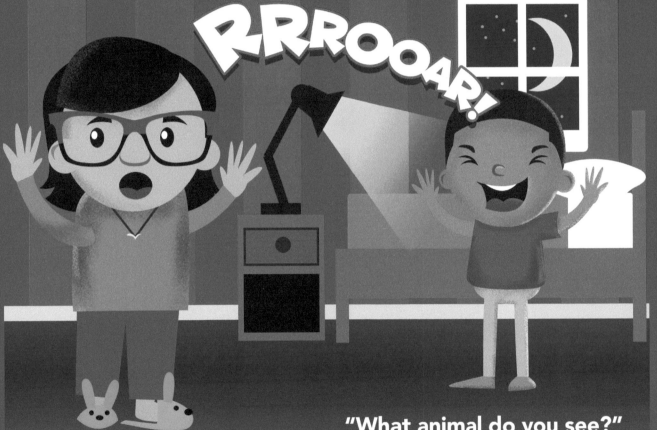

RRROOAR!

"What animal do you see?"
I screamed to the top of my lungs, "A lion, rrrooaaarrr!"
Titi got scared, but I know she was playing pretend.

"Tommy, do you know why I love lions?"
"Why Titi?"
"Lions remind me of one of Jesus' names in the Bible."

"What is it?"
"Jesus is the Lion of Judah.
Lions are strong, fearless, and majestic."

I was happy to learn that Jesus is strong
and majestic like a lion and fearless like a king.

The Lion from the tribe of Judah has won the victory. (Rev. 5:5b, ICB)

"Titi, what is the sound an ant makes?"
"Is that why you are looking down? Oh, there it goes!
I see it too!"

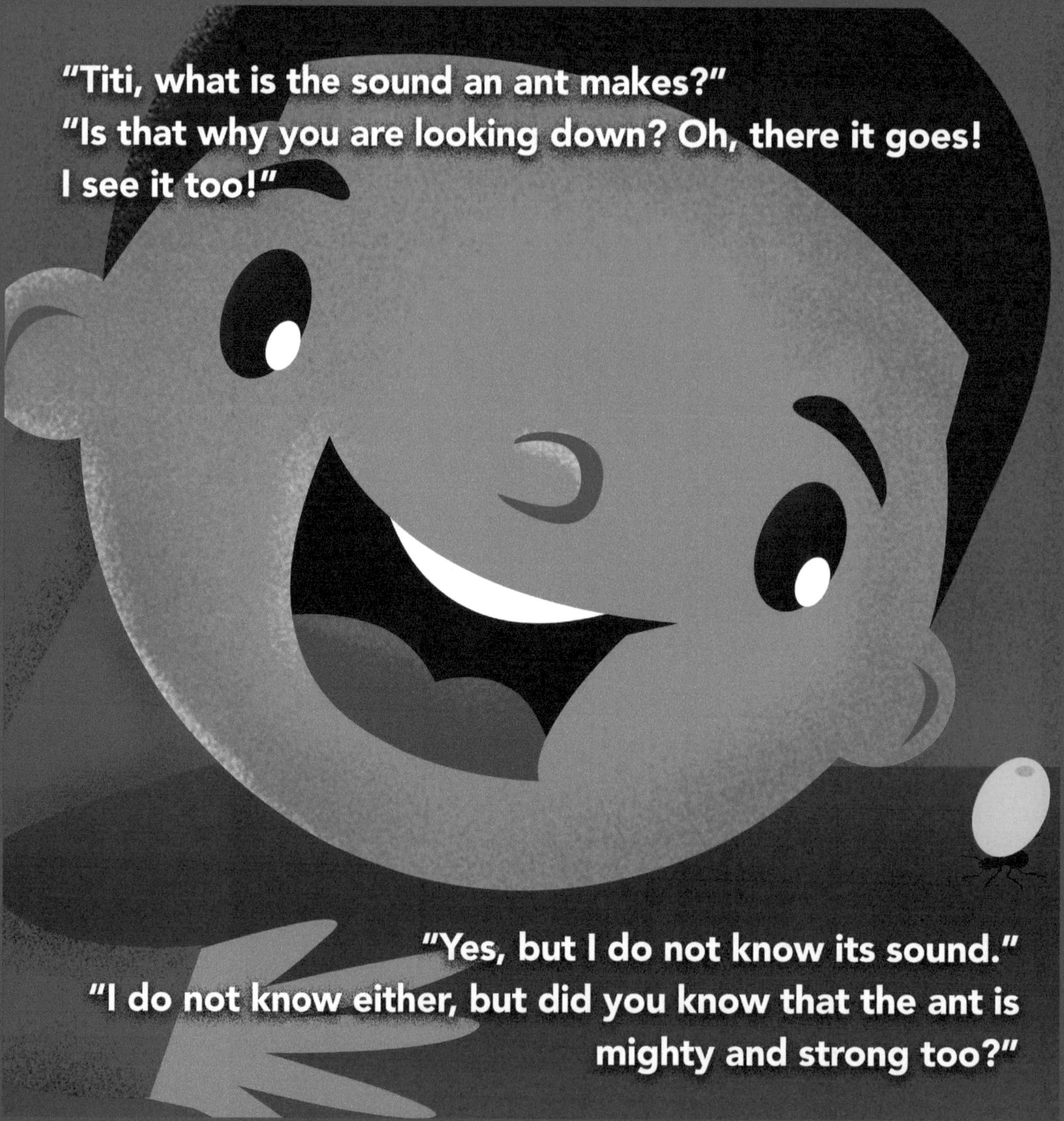

"Yes, but I do not know its sound."
"I do not know either, but did you know that the ant is
mighty and strong too?"

"But ants are so tiny. Can I step on it?"

"No Tommy! It is working hard. Instead of being lazy, it is gathering food for the next season and storing it up before the winter comes. Do you organize and store your meals?"

"No Titi, I am too little for that. My mommy does that for me."

Ants do serious work. I want to be strong and hardworking just like the ant.

Go watch the ants... Watch what they do and be wise (Prov. 6:6, ICB)

"Tommy look! It's a deer!"
"Wow Titi, it jumps so high! Look at it climb!
Is it thirsty? It was running fast to get to the water, Titi."
"Yes, Tommy. The deer runs to the water like we should run to God, with all our might."

If I were a deer, I would run to God, and I would want to hug Him. I wonder what that would look like.

A deer thirsts for a stream of water. In the same way, I thirst for you, God. (Prov. 42:1, ICB

"Oo oo oo, ah ah ah, oo oo oo, ah ah ah!"
"Tommy, why are you jumping around like a monkey?"
"I am playing monkey see, monkey do with the
monkey over there."
"Oh, I see. The monkey looks like it is happy."

AH AH AH!

"Titi, I know another word for happy. It is joy!"
"That is correct! Good job Tommy."
"Does the Bible talk about monkeys?"
"Well, it talks about King Solomon receiving apes and baboons as gifts and treasures. They are kind of like monkeys."

"That makes me sad."
"I am sorry Tommy. However, the Bible does talk about joy."
"Really Titi!"
"It sure does. Now together, let us be joyful like a monkey."

So Titi and I started to jump for joy like the monkey,
"Oo oo oo, ah ah ah, oo oo oo, ah ah ah!"
I want to be joyful, like the monkey!

Be joyful because you have hope. (Rom. 12:12, ICB)

I followed Titi's eyes go up, and up, and up and there we saw...
"... a giraffe. Over there Tommy, it is a beautiful giraffe. Look at its long, lovely neck."

"Titi, why is the neck so long."
"This is how they can see over the trees and see what's coming. It is like sticking out their neck for a friend."

"The long neck looks so silly Titi."
"It is kind of silly, right? It is also the way they can eat from the trees. You want to know something else?"
"Yes, Titi."
"Giraffes have a huge heart."
"How big is it?"
"It is almost as big as you."
"Wow! Why? Maybe it loves all his friends a lot."

"Well, that is a possibility. The reason it needs a big heart is so the heart can push and pump the blood up and down the giraffe's neck so that it can reach its brain."
I want a big heart like the giraffe, but not to eat from trees. I do not eat trees. I want a big heart, so I can give my family and friends big hugs.

A friend loves you all the time. (Prov. 17:17, ICB)

"Yawn..."
"Tommy you are getting sleepy. Time for bed."
"Ah, but I am not... yawn, sleepy."

"Oh, I think you are."
Titi always tucks me in, and as she gave me my goodnight hug and kiss, I saw another animal.

"Titi?"
"Yes, Tommy."
"I see one more animal."
"Oh, you do? Where?"
"Right there on your neck."
"My necklace? That is a dove."

"It looks beautiful Titi. It looks like the dove in the story
we read in the last sleepover. Jesus was baptized by
John the Baptist. That is Jesus' cousin right Titi?"
"Yes, he was. Good job remembering that!"

"Yeah, so John the Baptist baptized Jesus in the water, the clouds opened up, God the Father spoke and the dove came from the sky. The dove is the Holy Spirit, right Titi?"

Jesus was baptized and came up out of the water. Heaven opened, and he saw God's Spirit coming down on him like a dove. (Matt. 3:16 ICB)

"That is correct Tommy. I am so proud that you remember, however, it is time to say your prayers and go to sleep."

"Alright, Titi. Dear Jesus, we thank you for this beautiful day, and we thank you for our family and friends... Mommy, Daddy, Louie, Izzy, Mama, Papa, Tio, Tia Alexa, Gideon, Lucia, Nana, Titi, Rebekah, Sammy, and Brick City Church. Amen."

"Goodnight Thomas."
"Wait! I forgot to pray for the animals. Dear Jesus, bless the lion, the ant, the deer, the monkey, and the giraffe. Amen."

"You did not pray for the dove."
"Titi, remember, that is because the dove blesses us."
"Yes, the Holy Spirit blesses us. Now, in Jesus name we pray..."
And together Titi and I said, "Amen."

"Titi?"
"Last thing Tommy."
"Can I tell the people in church on Sunday about the dove, you know the Holy Spirit?"
"Why?"

"Everyone needs to know about the dove so they can be happy and calm like me."
"I think that is a good idea, Tommy."

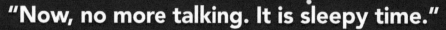

"Now, no more talking. It is sleepy time."
"Bendicion, Titi."
"Dios te bendiga Tommy."

I always say "Bendicion Titi." That is asking my Titi to pray a blessing over me in Spanish. She says, "Dios te bendiga." That is Spanish for "May God Bless you."

I go to bed and sleep in peace. Lord, only you keep me safe. (Psalm 4:8, ICB)

CPSIA information can be obtained
at www.ICGtesting.com
Printed in the USA
BVHW021230110319
542309BV00001B/12/P